This book belongs to

. . . .

KT-500-366

C0000 020 197 324

LADYBIRD BOOKS

UK | USA | Canada | Ireland | Australia | India | New Zealand | South Africa

Ladybird Books is part of the Penguin Random House group of companies
whose addresses can be found at global.penguinrandomhouse.com.

www.penguin.co.uk   www.puffin.co.uk   www.ladybird.co.uk

Penguin
Random House
UK

First published 2020
001

This book copyright © Astley Baker Davies Ltd/Entertainment One UK Ltd 2020
Adapted by Lauren Holowaty

This book is based on the TV series *Peppa Pig*.
Peppa Pig is created by Neville Astley and Mark Baker.
Peppa Pig © Astley Baker Davies Ltd/Entertainment One UK Ltd 2003.
www.peppapig.com

Printed in China

A CIP catalogue record for this book is available from the British Library

ISBN: 978-0-241-41197-1

All correspondence to:
Ladybird Books
Penguin Random House Children's
80 Strand, London WC2R 0RL

FSC
www.fsc.org

MIX
Paper from
responsible sources
FSC® C018179

Super Peppa!

It was 'All About Me' week at playgroup.
"Now, children," began Madame Gazelle, "I'd like you to start by each drawing a picture of yourself."
"Oooh!" cried Peppa and her friends, grabbing the paints, crayons and glitter.

All About Me

When they'd finished, they put their pictures on the wall.
"We look very important up on the wall," said Peppa proudly.
"You are very important," replied Madame Gazelle.
"I'm a bit wonky!" said Suzy Sheep, giggling.

Next, Madame Gazelle asked the children to think about what they all liked to do.

"I like bouncing," said Zoe Zebra, jumping up and down.

Hee! Hee! Hee!

"I like standing on one leg," said Freddy Fox, trying to balance.

"I like laughing," said Candy Cat, rolling on the floor and giggling.

HOOOWWWWLLL

"I LIKE HOWLING REALLY LOUDLY!" howled Wendy Wolf.

"Lovely," said Madame Gazelle. "You all like to do lots of different things."

"Now think about what you're good at," said Madame Gazelle, "and what you want to be when you grow up."

"I'm good at being clever," said Edmond Elephant. "I'm going to be an astronaut **and** an anthropologist."

"I'm good at being brave," said
Danny Dog. "I'm going to be
a champion skateboarder.
Whoosh!"

"I'm good at eating
carrots!" cried
Rebecca Rabbit.
"I'm going to be,
er . . . a carrot?"

"Next week, I'd like you to come dressed as
what you want to be when you grow up,"
said Madame Gazelle.

Hee!

Peppa put up her hand. "But I don't know what I want
to be." She sighed. "How will I know what to dress up as?"

"Don't worry, Peppa," said Madame Gazelle. "You can dress up as anything you like. Even a carrot." Everyone giggled.

"But how do I choose?" asked Peppa.
"Why don't you talk to some grown-ups to see what they do?"
suggested Madame Gazelle. "They can help you decide."
"OK," said Peppa.

Just then, the doorbell rang and it was time
to go home.
"Goodbye, everyone," said Madame Gazelle.
"See you next week."
"Goodbye, Madame Gazelle!" called
the children.

The next day, Peppa asked
Mummy Pig about her work.
"I write my stories on the
computer," explained Mummy Pig.
"When I think of an idea,
I go like this . . ."
Mummy Pig wrote an amazing
story and read it to Peppa.

Tap!
Tap!
Tap!

"Wow, Mummy! I want to be a writer just like you," said Peppa. "You write super stories!"
"You **can** be a writer, Peppa," said Mummy Pig. "Why don't you try writing a story now?"

"But what if I can't think of a story?" asked Peppa.
"You have to believe you can," said Mummy Pig.
"But what if people don't like it?" asked Peppa.
"You have to **believe** they will," said Mummy Pig.

"OK," said Peppa, and she told Mummy Pig a wonderful story about a princess, a frog and a little prince.

"What a **super** story!" said Mummy Pig. "You see, Peppa, when you believe you can do something, it helps you do it."

After lunch, Daddy Pig took Peppa to his muddy-puddle-jumping competition.
"I hope you win, Daddy," Peppa whispered.
"I might," replied Daddy Pig. "I am a bit of an expert."

Daddy Pig leapt high up into the air and landed with a perfect splash!

He won the golden cup and the crowd cheered. "Hooray for Daddy Pig!"
"Wow, Daddy! I want to jump in competitions just like you,"
cried Peppa. "You're a super muddy-puddle-jumper!"

"Why don't you try jumping now, Peppa?"
said Daddy Pig.
"But I'm not an expert like you," replied Peppa.
"You can be an expert," said Daddy Pig.
"You just have to practise."
Daddy Pig helped Peppa
practise jumping.

Then, Peppa leapt high up into the air and made an enormous SPLASH! The crowd were covered in mud, and they cheered and cheered. "Hooray for Peppa!"

"That was amazing! Thank you, Daddy," said Peppa.

Next, Peppa went to see Miss Rabbit.
"I hope you're ready for a busy day, Peppa!" Miss Rabbit cried.
Peppa followed her as she zoomed from one job to the next.

They raced from the supermarket . . .

to the fire station . . .

on to the museum . . .

and then to the theatre.

After that, Miss Rabbit took some visitors for a helicopter ride . . .

and sold everyone some yummy ice creams!

"Wow, Miss Rabbit! I want to be just like you and do lots of things," said Peppa, as Miss Rabbit drove everyone home on the train. "You're super at EVERYTHING!"

"If you work hard, you can be good at anything,"
said Miss Rabbit.
"Do I work hard?" asked Peppa.
"Yes," replied Miss Rabbit. "You've been working hard with
me all afternoon. You're super at everything, just like me!"

But when she got home, Peppa was confused. She still didn't know who to dress up as for playgroup. "Mummy, Daddy and Miss Rabbit are super at **everything**, George. And I want to be just like them. But how can I dress up as 'everything'?"

"Soo-pa Po-tay-to!" cheered George,
soaring his toy through the air.
"That's it, George!" cried Peppa, having a clever idea.
She headed straight to her dressing-up box . . .

The next day at playgroup, all the children were dressed up.
"I see you decided to be a superhero, Peppa," said Madame Gazelle.
"I'm not a superhero," replied Peppa. "I am . . . SUPER!"

"Mummy, Daddy and Miss Rabbit said if
you believe in yourself, practise and work
hard you can be super at anything.
And I do, so I'm Super Peppa!"

"Wonderful, Peppa!" said Madame Gazelle.
"I mean . . . super!"
"Super Peppa!" everyone cheered,
racing over to the dressing-up box.

When they came back, they were all wearing
super costumes, just like Peppa!
Mummy Pig, Daddy Pig and Miss Rabbit had
helped Peppa to be super.

And now Peppa had helped everyone
else to be super, too.
"Super Peppa. Super everyone!"
announced Madame Gazelle, swishing
her cape from side to side.

"We are all super!"